Dick Whittington is twelve years old.
He likes stories. Here he is.
He is listening to stories of London.
They are his favourite stories!

Dick sees a man and a horse.
'Hello!' Dick says, 'I am going to London.'
'Jump in!' the man says, 'my horse can walk
quickly!'

2

'London is big!' Dick says.
He walks and walks . . . and walks.
He looks at the children in London.
They have got sad faces.

Dick is hungry. He sits down next to a
beautiful house and goes to sleep.

'Hello. Who are you?' a man asks.
'Come in.'

'This is my house.
My name is Mr Smith,' the man says.

'This is Alice.'
'Hello Alice,' Dick says.
'Hello Dick,' Alice says.

There are mice in Dick's bedroom but there is a cat too! The cat is his friend. It catches the mice and eats them quickly!

Later Mr Smith says,
'Please give me your cat, Dick.
'He can go to sea with my friend Harry.'
'Mmmm,' the cat says, 'a holiday!'

In a far-off country, Harry meets the king's friends.
'Please come to dinner at the king's castle this evening,' they say.

At the castle, the men eat and eat. It is a big dinner.
'Oh, no, look,' the king says, 'it is the mice again!'

Harry gets Dick's cat for the king.
Dick's cat runs . . . and jumps!
'Good!' the king says, 'the cat is
catching the mice.'

'Miaaaow!' the cat says, 'I like mice!'
'Mmmm,' he says, 'one, two, three, four, five.
This is my big dinner!'

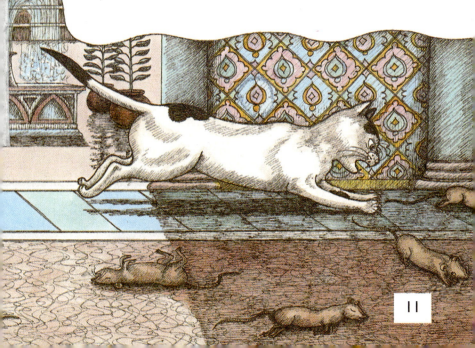

'Your cat lives in a far-off country now,'
Mr Smith says to Dick.
'Here are presents from the king.'
'Oh!' Dick says, 'they're beautiful!'

'Alice', Dick says, 'you are beautiful!'
'Dick,' Alice says, 'you are handsome!'
'Let's get married,' Dick says.
'Oh, we're happy,' they say.

Now Dick is old. He is a good man. He has got a school in London.
Today the children there have got happy faces!

# ACTIVITIES

BEFORE YOU READ

Look at the pictures in Dick Whittington.
Answer the questions: yes or no.

Page 1
1. Is the boy in the countryside?
2. Is he watching television?

Page 3
3. Is the boy in a beautiful town?
4. Are the children in the town happy?

Page 6
5. Can you see a cat?

Pages 8–9
6. Is the boy in the pictures?

Page 12
7. Is the boy sad?

AFTER YOU READ
There are five words in the square: Dick, cat, happy,
king, mice.
Can you find them?

```
E  C  I  M  H
K  I  N  G  A
C  P  T  K  P
H  C  A  T  P
D  I  C  K  Y
```

Edinburgh Gate, Harlow,

ISBN 0 582 43094 1

First published by Librairie du Liban Publishers, 1996
This adaptation first published 2000 under licence by Penguin Books

© 2000 Penguin Books Limited
Illustrations © 1996 Librairie du Liban

1 3 5 7 9 10 8 6 4 2

Series Editors: Annie Hughes and Melanie Williams
Dick Whittington, Level 1, retold by Marie Crook
Illustrated by Francesca Duffield
Designed by Jock Graham

Printed in Scotland by Scotprint, Musselburgh

Published by Pearson Education Limited in association with Penguin Books Ltd,
both companies being subsidiaries of Pearson Plc

For a complete list of the titles available in the Penguin Young Readers series
please write to your local Pearson Education office or to:
Marketing Department, Penguin Longman Publishing,
5 Bentinck Street, London W1M 5RN